Mother Bear's Scarf

Story by Beverley Randell
Illustrations by Isabel Lowe

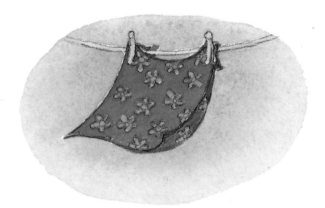

Rigby®

A Harcourt Achieve Imprint

www.Rigby.com
1-800-531-5015

2

One day
Father Bear and Baby Bear
went down to the river.

Mother Bear stayed at home.

4

"I will wash my red scarf today," said Mother Bear.

She washed the towels, too. "They will dry in the sun and the wind," she said.

Mother Bear went inside.

The red scarf and the towels went flying away in the wind.

"Where is my red scarf?"

said Mother Bear.

"I **liked** my red scarf.

And where are the towels?"

"I can see the towels,"
said Mother Bear.
"They are up in the trees!"

"Oh where is my red scarf?"
she cried.
She walked on,
down to the river.

"I can see a red fish
coming down the river,"
shouted Baby Bear.

"I will get it," he said.

"I'm good at fishing."

"This is not a **fish**!"

said Baby Bear.

"Look!

It is Mother Bear's red scarf."

"You **are** good at fishing,"

said Mother Bear.